בס"ד
לד' הארץ ומלואה

This book belongs to:

Please read it to me!

Happy Birthday to Me!
(Girls' Edition)

To my children, who bring such joy. C.L.

Children's children are a crown to the aged, and parents are the pride of their children. (Proverbs 17: 6)
I dedicate this book to my parents, and to the memory of my grandparents. P.A.

First Edition February 2006 - Shevat 5766
Second Impression November 2009 - Kislev 5770
Third Impression February 2014 – Adar 1 5774
Copyright © 2006 by HACHAI PUBLISHING
ALL RIGHTS RESERVED

Editor: Devorah Leah Rosenfeld
Managing Editor: Yossi Leverton
Layout: Moshe Cohen

ISBN-13: 978-1-929628-31-5
ISBN-10: 1-929628-31-5
LCCN: 2005937233

HACHAI PUBLISHING
Brooklyn, New York
Tel: 718-633-0100 Fax: 718-633-0103
www.hachai.com info@hachai.com

Printed in China

Glossary
Bracha - blessing
Mitzva - one of the 613 commandments; a good deed
Parsha - Torah portion read each week on Shabbat
Tehillim - Psalms
Torah - Jewish Scripture and Oral Tradition; the Five Books of Moses
Tzedaka - charity

Happy Birthday To Me!

By Channah Lieberman • Illustrated by Patti Argoff

Leah clapped her hands
and danced a little jig.
Today was the day!
She was getting so big!

"I'll go and tell Mommy it's my birthday today,"
But she seemed so busy, that Leah went away.

"I'll call and tell Father!"
Leah dialed the phone,
But a busy signal
made her feel so alone.

"My sisters and my brothers,
they probably forgot
I'll go and remind them...
Oh, well. Maybe not."

HAPPY BIRTHDAY

"What if no one remembers
today is my day?
I'll have to remind them
in my very own way!"

She noticed some paper hats
high on a shelf
And asked, "Mom, can I
make a party all by myself?"

"Take whatever you need;
I'll be there soon,"
Her mother called back
from the other room.

With a bump and a thump, Leah skipped down the hall
And knocked something heavy right off of the wall.

The tzedaka box fell and
landed on the ground,
Which gave Leah
the greatest idea around.

"My friends can throw in coins. We'll toss them from far.
Whoever gets the most will be the Mitzva Super Star."

"Now at my party we'll need something to eat
So we can make a bracha and have a treat."
She hurried to the kitchen to see what she could find,
Wow! A chocolate cake, her favorite kind!

With the hats and tzedaka box
under her arm,
Leah balanced the cake
so it wouldn't come to harm.

As she passed the freezer, the door was open wide.
   And what do you know? There was ice cream inside!
"Just what I need for my party today,"
   So Leah scooped it up and went on her way.

She held ice cream in one hand
and cake in the other,
The tzedaka box and hats
were really heavy. Oh brother!

Right there on the counter
in a pile so neat,
Lay her papers from school
and her parsha sheet.

"That's it!" Leah cried.
"I know what else to do.
I'll tell my friends the parsha
and some Jewish stories, too."

With papers in her mouth,
  and hats on her head
She put the tzedaka box
  in her pocket instead.

The ice cream made her hands red and freezing cold.
So the chocolate cake got really hard to hold.

Leah turned around
    and then stopped to stare
At a bag of shiny coins
    on a kitchen chair.

She couldn't imagine
    who had time to prepare
Those tzedaka pennies
    for her to share!

Leah tucked the bag of coins
right under her chin
She pressed her lips together
to keep the papers in.

With the hats still in place, tzedaka box in her skirt
The ice cream and cake made her hands start to hurt.

But Leah was happy; it was time for some fun –
Then she realized, "I haven't invited anyone!"

Her thrill disappeared like air from a balloon,
Friends wouldn't be coming over any time soon.

Then BAM, BOOM, CRASH –
the door flew open wide,
All the neighborhood kids
smiled and rushed inside.

Such excitement and joy
shone in Leah's eyes,
Her family had planned
this birthday surprise!

Just then, the tzedaka box
started to slip,
And the ice cream container
started to drip.
Leah lost her balance
and started to trip...

The papers flew around;
coins rolled on the ground,
And the cake fell – plop –
with Leah on top!

There was chocolate on her nose and icing in her ear
But the party wasn't ruined – so, never fear!
Everything was better than she
    could have wished...

...Even though the cake
    got a little bit squished!

There were Torah stories and Jewish songs to sing,

They all said a bracha and ate every last thing.

They stuffed the tzedaka box
   full to the top,
Tossing coin after coin,
   they didn't want to stop!

Leah picked a mitzva to do better than before,
  She decided to listen to her parents even more.

Everybody said Tehillim all together out loud
  Then the birthday girl stood up and said to the crowd,
"Thank you for coming. Now I know just what to do –
  Let's make a birthday party like this for each of you!"

There were Torah stories and Jewish songs to sing,

They all said a bracha and ate every last thing.

They stuffed the tzedaka box
   full to the top,
Tossing coin after coin,
   they didn't want to stop!

Leah picked a mitzva to do better than before,
She decided to listen to her parents even more.

Everybody said Tehillim all together out loud
Then the birthday girl stood up and said to the crowd,
"Thank you for coming. Now I know just what to do –
Let's make a birthday party like this for each of you!"

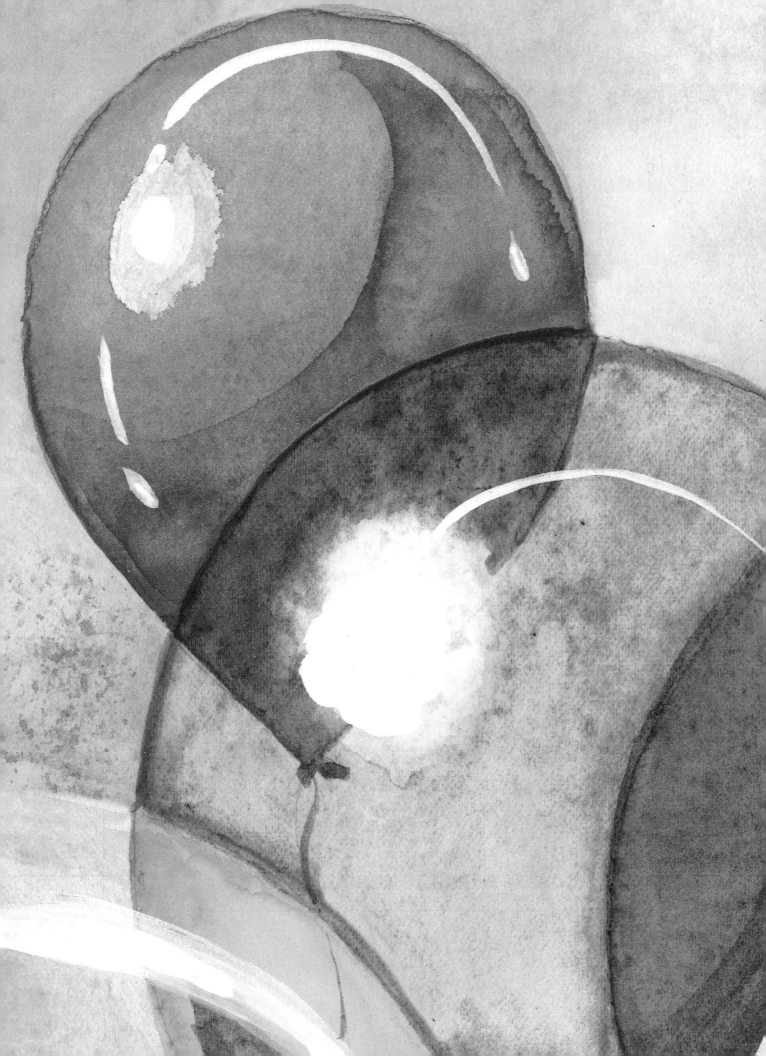